Faerie Tail

A Short Story for All Ages

Faerie Tail -
A Short Story for All Ages
by Becca Bates
Published by Indie Artist Press
Eagle Mountain, Utah
www.indieartistpress.com
First Edition
ISBN 978-1-62522-075-2
copyright © 2015 Becca Bates
All rights reserved.
October 2015

This is a work of fiction. Names, places, businesses, characters and incidents are either the product of the author's imagination or are used in a fictitious manner. Any resemblance to actual persons, living or dead, actual events or locales is purely coincidental.

Publisher's Note

Thanks for taking the time to enjoy *Faeiry Tail* by fantasy author Becca Bates. We know you'll enjoy this journey as much as we did.

If you haven't yet, we invite you to visit our website at *http://www.indieartistpress.com* where you'll find Becca's short story *A World Of My Own.*

An ebook version *of Faerie Tail* is available free at the author's website when you subscribe to her email newsletter.

You can visit the author at her website: http://beccabates.weebly.com.

Faerie Tail

Becca Bates

Indie Artist Press

Chapter One

Surprise, Surprise!

Once upon a time there lived a prince, which is typical of faerie tales. The prince's name was Elric, and he was engaged to be married. It was an arranged marriage, which is also common in faerie tales.

Elric wasn't sure what to think of the situation. He was nervous about marrying somebody he had never met, but there really wasn't anybody he knew that he wanted to marry anyway. And he was too short for any girls to be interested in him.

Besides, his parents had an arranged marriage, and they turned out alright. And from what he'd heard, Princess

Adelaide sounded like a decent girl, which was a plus, especially since she was a princess. Everybody knew how princesses could be. Or, at least how everybody *said* princesses could be.

Admittedly, Elric didn't have much experience with princesses. He had no sisters, and Regallin, the land he was from, was a bit hard to reach, so they didn't entertain many guests. The only princess he really knew was his sister-in-law Rose, but all she ever seemed to do was eat.

Elric wondered if his bride-to-be thought about anything other than food. He hoped so. While he didn't always show it, he really respected his brother Alonzo and knew that he'd be a great leader someday, even without any input from unconcerned wife. Elric, however, was less certain of his own capability.

Princess Adelaide was the only child of King Nathaniel and Queen Clarice – though Clarice was actually her stepmother, which Elric was naturally uneasy about;

he'd heard too many tales about wicked stepmothers – and marrying Adelaide would insure that someday he would replace Nathaniel as King of Malmor.

Nobody knew as well as Elric did how ironic that notion was. Clumsy, uncoordinated, slow-learning Elric was destined to become king of an entire country. Granted, it wasn't a very large country, but it was a still relatively new country. This Elric found even more unnerving than meeting a stepmother.

By becoming ruler of a newly developed country, not only would there be a lot of pressure on his shoulders to lay good foundations for future generations, but he would also always be listed near the beginning of the history of kings, so he'd be remembered a lot more easily than the future kings. He could never remember past about the third king in the history of Regallin.

Elric sighed, hoping Princess Adelaide would have better ideas about ruling a country than he did.

~*~

Princess Ada sighed, hoping she would have better luck with Prince Elric than she'd had with her last suitor. From the moment he'd first laid eyes on her, all he could do was stare. He'd awkwardly tried to carry on a conversation, but he was out the door as soon as he was able. He then told all the other possible suitors about his experience, and none of them were willing to come after that.

So, Ada had been sent back to Grandmother's House, where she had spent most of her childhood. She stayed there until her father had summoned her, saying that he had found someone to marry her. Of course, he also added the fact that she wouldn't meet the prince until the wedding. And of course, Ada knew why without him having to explain.

If the prince saw her before that, he wouldn't go through with the marriage. Ada wondered if he would stop the wedding in the middle once he saw her, despite her father's obvious opinion that Prince Elric wouldn't dare to.

Ada's attendant, Meleen, put a silver tiara – made specifically for Ada – on the princess's head, then stepped back off the stool and admired her finished work. Ada gazed at her reflection.

Just then, Queen Clarice entered the bedroom. She surveyed her stepdaughter and gave a nod of approval.

"Yes, that looks right," she said. "Come along, Ada. They should be here soon."

Ada followed her into the hallway, glancing back one last time at her reflection. The pair made their way to the empty sanctuary where the wedding was to take place.

Ada's tiara bumped into the low doorway, knocking it crooked.

"Oh, that won't do," Clarice said, hurrying to fix it. "You need to be careful. We must make a good impression on them."

Ada didn't think they would even look at the tiara. They'd be too distracted by the girl wearing it.

"Ah, there you are." King Nathaniel entered, followed by Pem, the messenger who had helped the two kingdoms make contact.

"My goodness, Ada, you look lovely," Pem said. That was what Ada liked about Pem. Even though he was technically hired help, he acted as though he were everybody's best friend.

"The watchmen have spotted a carriage approaching," Nathaniel said. "It will only be a few more minutes until they arrive. Where is the minister?"

"Getting dressed. He should be out shortly," Clarice answered.

"Good, then we're just about ready," Nathaniel remarked.

"Ready? But aren't you missing something?" Pem asked.

"Missing what?" Clarice asked.

"The guests!" Pem said. "You can't start the wedding before the guests arrive!"

Clarice and Nathaniel exchanged looks.

"Well, actually there are no guests. Other than Prince Elric's family, of course," Clarice replied.

"What? No guests? That's ridiculous! If I were a princess about to be married, why, I'd want the whole country at my wedding!"

The king and queen stared at Pem in wonder. Could he really be so naïve?

"Oh, look!" Clarice exclaimed, thankful for the distraction. "The minister is here. Let's get in our places. Pem, you go meet the groom and his family and bring them here. As soon as they arrive, the wedding will start."

~*~

As the carriage rumbled through the gateway and entered the country, Elric pulled back the curtain of the window and looked for the first time at his future kingdom. A frown quickly formed on his face.

"It's so small!" he said.

"Yes, it's a small country. You knew that already," his mother said without taking her eyes off the book she was reading.

"No, I mean the buildings are small," Elric said. Now curious, his family looked out as well. Sure enough, unlike the grand, large buildings and houses of Regallin, everything here was small and dainty. Too small, in fact.

"How can anyone live in a house that small?" Elric asked. "Wouldn't they be cramped in there? Unless . . ."

As soon as the thought entered his mind it was proved true, for just then he noticed the people. A feeling of dread swept over him. What was he getting himself into? They were all almost half as tall as the people in Regallin, some less.

The townspeople saw the carriage and stopped whatever they were doing to stare. They were just as surprised at the large size of it as Elric was at the small size of the town.

Elric looked at his parents to see what

they thought. Maybe they would call off the wedding, and he wouldn't have to live in the tiny place. He was already a klutz; he could only imagine how clumsy he'd be when he had to duck under every doorway. But though his parents shared a frown of doubt, they seemed to be resigned to the fact. They both knew that there wouldn't be many chances to get Elric married off. They weren't going to stop the wedding.

The carriage rolled to a stop in front of the palace.

"Well, Elric, I guess there's finally a good reason you're so short," Alonzo teased. Elric glared at him. He wasn't anywhere near *that* short!

The carriage door opened and the messenger bowed.

"Welcome to the lovely country of Malmor," he said with a bow. "Pem Puk, at your service."

"We know who you are, Pem," Alonzo said.

"I know," Pem said. "I was trying to be

formal. Anyway, you are to come with me to the chapel. The service is all ready to get started. The only thing we're waiting for is you."

"Wait, you mean we're doing the wedding *now?*" Elric asked.

"Well, of course. Why wait? You're all here, and this is what you came for, isn't it? Now come on, let's go."

The family exited the carriage and followed Pem into the sanctuary. To Elric's surprise, it was empty except for the minister, whose eyes widened at their entrance, and a quartet.

"Where are the guests?" Elric whispered to Pem. It felt like a place where you needed to whisper.

"I asked the same thing," Pem said. "Apparently, the king and queen wanted a small wedding."

"Yeah, a small everything," Elric mumbled.

"What was that?" Pem asked.

"Nothing," Elric said.

"Get in your place up on stage," Pem told him. As Elric hesitantly walked to the stage, Pem seated his family in the front row. Once Elric was in place the quartet began to play. The door in the back of the sanctuary opened and the king and queen entered.

As soon as they saw Elric's family, both froze, as did their twin smiles, horror filling their eyes. Pem waved them on, and they reluctantly walked down the aisle and sat opposite the Regallins.

The music changed, and everyone turned to see the bride as she ducked under the doorway. Yes, she had to duck, for to Elric's greatest surprise of the day, Princess Adelaide was the tallest person in Malmor. Though she wasn't quite as tall as the average Regallin, Elric guessed that she would come up to his shoulder, which was extraordinarily tall compared to the other Malmords he had seen. But how could someone so short have a child who was so tall?

Ada was careful this time to duck low enough that her tiara wouldn't hit it again. As she lifted her head, she saw

Prince Elric on stage, and her jaw dropped. He was even taller than her, and his family appeared taller still! Her parents had been so negative about her height; she couldn't imagine what they must think of her groom. Judging by their expressions, they were the ones who wanted to call off the wedding but didn't have the nerve to.

The irony of the whole situation made Ada want to laugh. All her life her parents had been ashamed of her height, and now they had accidentally forced her to marry a giant because of it! She couldn't stop herself from releasing a small smile.

Elric watched as Adelaide's face changed first to surprise, and then to a slight smile. She seemed to be the only person in the room who was humored by the change of expectation. Except maybe Pem. Elric took this as a good sign. At least someone in this country wouldn't look down on his height – so to speak.

As soon as Princess Adelaide arrived

on podium, the minister began the ceremony. It seemed to be going by surprisingly fast – perhaps it was because the minister wanted it to be over as soon as possible – and Elric found himself saying "I do," almost before he realized they had gotten that far. And then it was Princess Adelaide's turn.

"Do you, Princess Adelaide, take Prince Elric to be your lawfully wedded husband?" the minister asked.

Adelaide looked Elric straight in the eye and said, with full confidence, "I do."

"You may now kiss the bride."

Elric gulped. With everything that had happened, he'd forgotten about the kiss. Even Adelaide looked nervous for the first time. Elric awkwardly leaned toward her. At the same time Adelaide took a step forward, suddenly closer to Elric then he had anticipated, and their foreheads collided, in classic Elric clumsiness.

They both reeled back, rubbing their foreheads. Elric could feel his brother's I-knew-this-was-bound-to-happen look from behind him.

Nobody seemed to know what to do next, so the minister decided to end the ceremony.

"I now pronounce you man and wife," he said.

King Nathaniel jumped to his feet. "Alright everyone, it's time for dinner. Let us proceed to the dining room."

Rose, at the mention of food, hopped up to follow. Everyone else walked to the room as if in a daze.

Since the ceremony had been hastened by the minister, dinner wasn't quite ready yet. The two families sat in their designated places around the empty table, the Regallins shifting to find the most comfortable position on the seats that were much to small for them, and Pem went to the kitchen to let them know that everyone was ready to eat.

Glass shattered, and everyone turned to see a servant had dropped a pitcher of water. She stood frozen for a moment until King Nathaniel cleared his throat loudly, reminding her of her job. She took off into the kitchen to get a broom, and the servants she passed wondered what she was so distressed about.

Another servant entered the dining room carrying a platter with several salad plates on it. He managed to steady the platter before it tipped, but his face betrayed his worry. He eyed Rose, wondering if they had enough food to feed her alone, never mind the rest of the giants. He would have to tell the cook to prepare more food, perhaps make up another course.

The rest of the dinner passed mostly in silence. It wasn't long before the entire kitchen knew what was going on, so there were no more casualties caused by surprise. As for the dinner party, none of them were sure what to say.

Elric found himself wishing Pem had joined them for dinner. He always seemed to have a way of lifting the tension. In any case, everyone was in a hurry to be out of this awkward situation, so the dinner passed rather swiftly.

Elric's mother then claimed that they were all tired after their journey, and asked to be shown to the rooms they were staying in for the night. Once they were led out of the dining room, Queen Clarice declared that she should get ready for bed, too, and her husband volunteered to join her, despite the fact that the sun hadn't even set yet. And then Elric and Adelaide were alone.

"So," Adelaide broke the silence, "would you like to see the rest of the castle?"

"I suppose," Elric said, then wondered if he should have said something more polite, like, *"Certainly,"* or, *"It would be a pleasure."* *"I suppose"* sounded like he was only willing because he had nothing better to do. Oh well, it was too late to change it now.

He stood up to follow Adelaide, grateful to finally get out of the tiny chair. Adelaide led him through the hallway, giving him a brief tour of the layout and pointing out various rooms. They headed upstairs, and Adelaide stopped at a door.

"This," she said, opening the door, "is our room."

Elric took in the room before him. Unlike the rest of the castle, it had a rather high ceiling and was more spacious than the other rooms he had seen.

"This room was added on," Adelaide explained. "It was designed specifically for me. And this is my favorite part."

She walked to the far side of the room where a pair of glass doors faced the forest outside. She opened the doors and stepped out on the balcony. Elric joined her.

"Mm, we made it just in time," Adelaide said.

Elric followed her gaze and saw the sun as it disappeared behind the trees. The colors of sunset painted the clouds and the trees.

Elric had never paid much attention to

sunsets before, but now he was blown away. He could see why Adelaide liked this spot so much. Perhaps this whole marriage situation wouldn't be so bad after all. Adelaide seemed to be just the kind of person he would want to spend his life with.

Chapter Two

To Grandmother's House They Go

Why didn't you say anything about it?!" Nathaniel asked. He had found Pem and was now taking out his anger.

"About what?" Pem asked, genuinely confused.

"About the fact that they're giants, of course! Surely you must have noticed!"

"Sure, I noticed, but it's not my place to judge. Besides, I think Elric and Ada will make a lovely pair. She'll finally have someone to look up to!"

Nathaniel groaned. "This is terrible! I can't have a giant ruling Malmor! Oh, what will the people think? What am I supposed to do now?"

"How about giving Elric a chance? I'm sure you'll like him once you get to know him."

"Why do I even bother talking to you?" Nathaniel muttered.

"Beats me! You obviously don't listen to anything I say," Pem said teasingly. "But then, I guess you won't have to bother much longer."

"What do you mean?" Nathaniel asked, his brow furrowing.

"Well, now that the wedding's over, there's not going to be as much contact between the two countries. You won't need me running back and forth through the forest anymore. So, I was going to take a vacation. I'm leaving tomorrow."

"Oh, well, I suppose that makes sense." Nathaniel was still a little taken aback by the news. "But what if Elric wants to talk to his family?" Nathaniel suddenly realized that it sounded as though he was trying to convince Pem to stay, and that made him wonder if he was trying to. The strange man always seemed to annoy him, but for some reason it seemed unreal to imagine life without him.

"No worries," Pem answered. "If he ever needs me, he can just call, and I'll be here right away."

It didn't make sense to Nathaniel, but then, hardly anything Pem said ever made sense.

~*~

"Wow, you really *are* tall!"

Elric turned to see a boy in the doorway.

"Who are you?" he asked.

"I'm Lachlan," the boy replied. "I've been assigned to be your personal servant."

"I see . . ."

"So, how tall are you, exactly?"

"Oh, I'm . . ." He was precisely eight and one-half feet, but normally in Regallin he would exaggerate a little and say he was eight-foot-seven. It made him seem a little closer to the average height, without being too far off from the truth.

But now he wanted to seem as short as possible. "Eight-foot-five."

Lachlan's eyes widened. "*EIGHT-foot-FIVE?!* I'm four-foot-eight! And people here never reach more than five-foot-four – well, *almost* never."

Elric knew who he was thinking of when he said that. Before anything else could be added, Adelaide, who had left the room shortly before Lachlan had arrived, returned.

"Oh, Lachlan," she said.

"Good evening, Princess Adelaide," he said, suddenly formal, even bowing.

Adelaide frowned. "What have you been up to?"

"Nothing," he said, eyebrows flying up toward the ceiling. "I was simply making my service known to your new husband."

"Mm-*hmm*," Adelaide said, but her eyes were laughing. "Well, you may be excused for the time being."

"Thank you," he said, giving another melodramatic bow. "Goodnight, Princess Adelaide, Prince Elric."

Lachlan turned and left the room, closing the door behind him.

"What was that all about?" Elric asked.

"Oh, Lachlan and I always tease each other," Adelaide explained. She saw Elric's disbelieving stare. "What?"

"It's just . . . I've never teased a servant before – and I've never seen a servant tease their master!"

"I see. Well, Lachlan's parents are our head servants, so I've known Lachlan since he was born. He's practically my little brother. Besides, I never had friends when I was little, so I was nice to the servants and some of them became my friends. Of course, not all of them liked me simply because–" Adelaide suddenly broke off and her face turned serious. "Anyway, I prefer to think of them as friends and family, rather than servants."

"Oh," Elric said. It was all he could think to say. And since he couldn't think of anything to add to the subject, he decided to change it. "So, where did you go just now?"

"I was making preparations for tomorrow," she said.

"What's happening tomorrow?"

"I'm sorry, I don't mean to spring this on you, but I couldn't think of a way to tell you before. I'm leaving tomorrow on a short trip. You can come, too, if you'd like. It would give us a chance to get to know each other better."

The idea of staying by himself at a small, unfamiliar place with people who seemed to be afraid of him sounded a million times worse than leaving on an unexpected trip with Adelaide. Besides, he hadn't even unpacked yet, so he was ready to go.

"I'd be happy to come. But where are we going? And why on such short notice?"

"Well, you see, I actually only lived at the palace until I was nine years old, and then briefly again when I was seventeen. I just arrived back here yesterday. The rest of the time, I spent at Grandmother's House in the woods. My father didn't give me much time to pack, and I left most of my things there. I promised to retrieve it myself."

"If Elric's going to Grandmother's House with you, does that mean I get to come, too?" Lachlan, who had apparently been eavesdropping, poked his head back into the room.

"That would be a logical conclusion," Adelaide said.

"Yes!" Lachlan exclaimed. "I gotta go pack!" And then he was gone for real.

There was a soft knock on the door.

"Come in," Adelaide called. A young woman stepped timidly into the room.

"Am I coming, too?" she asked. Her voice was so soft, Elric could barely hear her.

"Of course," Adelaide said. "You should pack, too."

The girl curtseyed before leaving.

"How many people are listening in?" Elric asked, exasperated.

"Probably just those two."

"Probably?"

"Hopefully."

"Who was that quiet girl?"

"Her name is Meleen. She's my Personal Attendant."

"I see," Elric said. "So it's just the four of us who are going, right?"

"Right."

~*~

"So, where does she live exactly?" Elric asked as they started out. Once again, Elric was grateful for Ada's – she had insisted he call her by her nickname – height, for she had had a custom built carriage that was almost as large as the ones in Regallin. He was much more comfortable than he expected.

"We just need to go over this river and through those woods. We should be there this evening."

What kind of Grandmother lives in the middle of the woods? Elric thought. But he didn't say anything – at least, not until they came to the river.

"*That's* a river?!" he exclaimed. "That's more like an ocean! I can hardly see the other side!"

Ada shrugged. "There is something you need to understand about Malmor. Here, it's 'the smaller, the better,' so even when something is big – like this river – they make it seem as small as possible."

Elric's stomach began to churn as he stared at the bridge they were approaching.

"Are you sure that bridge will be able to hold up under us?" he gulped.

"Oh, no doubt," Ada assured him. "It's the sturdiest bridge you'll ever find! It was built by the stone-workers and reinforced by faerie magic."

"Stone-workers? What are those? And faeries? They're just myths!" Elric said.

"Stone-workers are, what you would call, another 'myth,'" Ada replied, trying to stifle indignation at his ignorance – or perhaps it was at his disbelief. "They are the most gifted creatures in stone building. In fact, that is part of the faerie magic as well."

By this point, Elric was hardly paying attention because they were beginning to cross the bridge. He pulled his window shade closed and took a deep breath.

"What's wrong?" Ada asked. "Believe me, you don't have to worry about the bridge."

"It's not so much the bridge I'm worried about . . ."

"Then what is it?" Ada asked.

Elric hesitated, clenching his seat with all of his might. Lachlan, who until that moment had managed to keep his mouth shut due to a warning from Ada to watch what he said, finally could no longer hold his tongue.

"Wait a second. Don't tell me you're afraid of heights!"

Elric's cheeks flushed.

"But you can't be afraid of heights – you're a giant! You're too tall; you'd be afraid all the time!"

"Lachlan!" Ada cautioned.

"I'm not a giant!" Elric claimed. "You

are the ones that are too small – you're midgets!"

"We are not!" Lachlan argued.

"Boys, stop it," Ada said.

They both were quiet for a moment, then Elric mumbled, "I'm not a boy, either."

"Well, you were starting to act like one," Ada said. "But I do apologize."

"I'm sorry, too," Elric replied.

Silence filled the carriage. Finally, Ada said, "We're on the other side now."

Elric let out a sigh of relief and loosened his grip on his seat. He then, cautiously at first, pushed the curtain back and found that they were now in a path through the wood. For a while Ada and Elric chatted, with near constant interruption from Lachlan, and not a single interruption from Meleen. Elric told them about Regallin and Ada told him about Malmor.

After a couple of hours, they pulled over to stretch their legs. While Lachlan was off in the trees somewhere, Elric took advantage of the privacy (even with Meleen around, it felt private) to ask what he thought might be a more personal question.

"Ada," he said, "I heard that Clarice was your stepmother. May I ask what happened to your real mother?"

Ada looked down. "She died when I was seven. She got very sick."

"I'm sorry to hear that," Elric said. "I was wondering, though . . . Was she . . . was she from Malmor?" He wasn't sure how to ask what he wanted to.

"Yes, she was," Ada said.

"So, she wasn't . . . ." He didn't want to say "a giant," because he still didn't believe he was a giant. "Tall?"

"Oh, I see," Ada said with understanding. "You thought maybe I was tall because my mother was from Regallin, or some similar place. No, she was four-foot-two, actually one of the shortest women, and proud of it. We had no idea that there were really places like Regallin until yesterday. We'd heard rumors of so-called 'giants' but didn't think they existed. There is a reason for my height, but I won't tell you just yet."

"Why not?" Elric asked.

"You wouldn't believe me yet. But maybe tonight when we are at Grandmother's House I will tell you."

Elric was about to ask why she thought he wouldn't believe her now, but would believe her tonight, but just then Lachlan came back and they decided to keep going. A few hours later, Elric realized the answer for himself. Once they reached their destination, the first thing he saw out his window was a boy who appeared to be about seven or eight years old – only, he wasn't a normal boy. Though from the waist up he looked quite human, his legs were like those of a deer. Elric knew instantly that it was a faun, something he had heard stories about but never thought actually existed. He realized that he had let his jaw drop, and quickly closed his mouth so as not to appear rude.

"Does that look like a myth to you?" Ada asked teasingly as she pointed to a tiny ball of light that darted about in the air and flew up to the window. In the middle of the light was a figure similar to a human, but very, very small and with wings on her back. She could be no more than two inches in height.

"Is this your new husband, Ada?" she asked, her voice like the sound of bells.

"Yes, this is Elric," Ada said. "Elric, this is my friend Eámanë. She's a faerie."

"Nice to meet you," Eámanë said.

"Uh, it's nice to meet you, too," Elric stuttered. He couldn't believe that he was actually talking to a faerie – a real faerie!

"Ada's back!" came a shout from outside, and in a moment there was a great flutter and a clamor and the carriage came to a stop. Ada hopped out, quickly followed by Meleen.

"Come on!" Lachlan said, nudging Elric out the door. He dumbly obeyed and stumbled out of the carriage, tripping on the step and nearly crashing to the ground – in front of several more creatures of various shapes, sizes, and species.

"Oh, do be careful," Eámanë called. "Mind you, there are some of us about who are small enough to be trampled!"

"My apologies," Elric said, hanging his head.

The faerie giggled and flew to join in the commotion as everyone scrambled to wish Ada a fond welcome. She laughed and gave hugs to them all. Finally, after making sure she greeted everyone, she stepped back and said, "Everyone, I'd like you to meet my new husband, Prince Elric."

There was a chorus of "hellos" and "pleased to meet yous," to which Elric awkwardly waved and offered a self-conscious greeting in return.

"Oh, Ada, you made it!" The new voice came from the door to the house.

"Grandmother!" Ada cried and ran to embrace the wrinkled old woman.

"I'm sorry it took me so long to come

outside," she said. "I was entertaining a guest. Oh, that must be your husband. A fine-looking young man, he is."

"His name is Elric," Ada said. "And who is your guest?"

"Ada! Elric!" the guest cried in delight, emerging from the house. "I didn't realize you two were coming here!"

"Pem!" they both said in astonishment.

"What are you doing here?" Ada asked.

"Oh, Grandmother and I go way back," Pem said. "I decided to take a vacation, and thought I'd stop by here and visit an old friend. She always has the best tea, not to mention company, and it's been far too long since we last reconnected."

"Did you grow up at Grandmother's House, too?" Ada asked.

"Sadly, no," Pem said. "Though I would have loved to, had it been an option. It's wonderful, what she does here. But I do believe the tea is getting cold. Would you join us?"

"Certainly!" Ada agreed.

As they progressed to the house, Elric

whispered to her, "What exactly *does* she do here?"

"All the misfits and runaways and such, all who are lost, wind up here, where Grandmother cares for them and they become family," Ada explained. "Most that come are those who are wandering without a destination, but few, like me, came because their parents sent them."

"So . . . she's not actually your grandmother?" Elric asked.

"No," Ada said, "but she feels more like a true grandmother than a real one usually feels."

The company settled down in the dining room, which was much larger than Elric believed could belong in such a small house. There was plenty of room for everyone, and Elric noted that the ceiling was even high enough that he didn't have to duck. Grandmother poured tea for them all.

"So how long are you staying here?" Ada asked Pem.

"Oh, I haven't really thought about it yet," Pem answered. "I suppose I'll stay until I go. What about you? I do hope you'll stay for a while."

"Well, we just arrived, and it is already close to evening, so we will certainly be staying tomorrow. And it's such a long journey that it would only do to leave in the morning time, so we can't leave for at least two days. But . . . I, for one, would be quite delighted to stay longer. What do you think, Elric?"

"Uh, yes, that sounds . . . fine," he said, giving a weak smile. He wanted to like the place; he was just so startled by it that he would need time to adjust.

"Wonderful!" Pem cried with a clap of his hands.

"You can stay as long as you like," Grandmother assured her. "You're always welcome here."

And stay they did for two full days. Lachlan and Meleen had never been to the house, but had heard stories and were enamored by how incredibly better it was than even the stories had described. Though Meleen remained shyly to herself most of the time, Lachlan quickly fit in with the boys, getting into all sorts of mischief – all in fun, of course.

Ada showed Elric her favorite places and made a point to include him in all of her conversations with her old friends, and he soon felt much more comfortable around all of them. He had heard many legends of magical things in his youth, so he knew a lot about them, for most of the creatures there were magical in some way or another. It was rather like suddenly finding himself in the midst of his favorite story, and by the first night he almost forgot that he hadn't believed they even existed just one day before.

As much as they enjoyed their time there, they had nearly forgotten about leaving until the third morning when Pem suddenly cried out.

"Oh! Oh, my! Good heavens!"

"What is it?" Ada asked.

"Someone is in trouble!" he exclaimed.

"Who? Where?" Ada cried, looking about frantically for someone who might be hurt.

"If I'm not mistaken, I believe it's . . . no, that can't be! That's impossible!"

"What's impossible? Who is it?"

"The faerie queen!"

The whole room gasped.

"Where is she?" Grandmother asked.

"Very far away. Oh, I must be off at once!"

"But where are you going?" Elric asked.

"I don't know yet," Pem said. "But it doesn't matter."

"If she's in trouble, maybe we should come with you. Maybe we can help," Ada offered.

"Well, that's very generous of you, to be sure, but aren't you due back to your parents' house?" Pem replied.

"Oh, I'm sure they won't mind if we're gone a little while longer," Ada assured him. "In fact, they probably want us to take as long a trip as possible."

"If you're certain . . ." Pem said.

"Then it's settled," Elric said. "We'll gather our things and be off as soon as we can." He was willing to take any chance he could to postpone his inevitable fate of spending the rest of his life in a town full of people half his size. "Do you know how far away it is? How long should we expect to be gone?"

"It's impossible to say for sure," Pem said, tapping his chin in thought. "It's far away; could be a few days, could be a few weeks. But it isn't along the path, so we must travel by foot."

"Then we should send the carriage back with a message to my parents that we will be gone longer than expected, and that we will send for the carriage when we are ready to return," Ada declared. "Lachlan and Meleen will go with it."

"What? No!" Lachlan cried. "I want to go with you!"

"Lachlan . . ."

"Please? I'll behave and do everything you tell me to do, I promise! After all, I'm Elric's attendant. I'm supposed to go with him everywhere, aren't I?"

Ada and Elric exchanged looks.

"Well, I don't see a problem with him coming–" Elric had hardly finished when Lachlan whooped in delight and ran off to hastily pack his things. Meleen didn't ask, but figured that his permission was hers as well and quietly made her way to her own room to do the same.

And so it was that in just a little while the group set off into the woods with no idea of the direction or destination to which they were headed, with only Pem's intuition as their guide. With any other person, this would have seemed strange, but somehow it seemed quite natural to them that Pem would know this sort of thing, and they followed without question.

Chapter Three

The Dragon

The journey passed smoothly for some time. Despite being in an untamed wood, they never had trouble passing through. If Elric didn't know better, he would suspect that the wood itself was actually letting them through. Though there was no path cut, they never seemed to veer around the trees but always walked in a straight line. Once Elric looked back and saw a large tree directly behind them, one they would have had to detour around, but he could not recall it being in the way before. At night they rested under the trees on grass so soft that one could almost believe it was a mattress and pillow.

On the second day as they travelled through the never-ending trees, they heard a voice shout, "Lo! A Dragon! I shall cut you through!"

The group froze as the voice let out a long yell that travelled through the trees as though the yeller was running. Suddenly there was a high-pitched, "*a-CHOO!*" and the yell stopped. A moment later there came a low croak, though Elric could have sworn it sounded very much like the word, "WHAAaaaaaAATT?!"

The travelers ran toward the sounds and came into a small clearing where they saw a very large lizard, and a very small frog sitting on a sword. The frog held its front legs in front of its eyes, and then attempted to look at the rest of his body, failing miserably as it wound up hopping in circles.

Meanwhile, the lizard, who was about as long as Elric was tall, said, in a slightly hissing voice, "Oh, no, not another one. Let me guess, a prince and his company come to slay the dragon and win the fair princess' heart."

Elric was a bit startled by the lizard's ability to speak, and also the fact that it was clearly a female voice, but recovered quickly and replied, "No, not at all. I mean, I am a prince, but I have no intention of slaying dragons. And I've already married a princess."

"Oh, that's good news," the lizard said. "Sorry if I came off as rude; it can get very tiring being chased by princes all the time."

At this point, the frog had finally given up hopping about and let his long tongue roll out, which seemed to prove to him that he was, in fact, a frog. "Now Sera will never marry me," he croaked. He turned to the lizard and shook his fist – or, at least the frog equivalent of a fist, which isn't very much like a fist at all – at her and cried, "You haven't seen the last of me, beast! I shall return, and you shall meet your end!"

After this he hopped away into the woods. As he did, there came another "a-

choo!" and there was a puff of pollen from a nearby flower. A small light emerged, and a faerie shook herself of the pollen and sneezed again.

"Ugh, I'm allergic to pollen, too!" she moaned, then faced the lizard. "What happened to the prince?"

"He turned into a frog," she answered. "What were you trying to do?"

"Uh, nothing big just . . . turn his sword into a harmless flower, but . . . oh, well," the faerie said, clearly put out by her mistake.

"At least it was the same *type* of spell this time," the lizard encouraged. "You're getting better."

"Oh, who are they?" the faerie exclaimed as she saw the travelers. "Not another fight!" She began to twirl her arm in the air, causing faerie dust to swirl, but the lizard cut her off.

"No, they aren't trying to fight," she said.

"Really? That's great!" the faerie cried in relief, then let out another sneeze, which sent her flying back a foot.

"Pardon Leilani," the lizard said to the travelers. "She's allergic to faerie dust."

"That must be hard," Ada sympathized.

"It is," Leilani replied, "but you learn to manage."

"My name is Ada, and this is my husband Elric and our friends Pem, Lachlan, and Meleen."

"I'm Leilani," she said. "And that is Raja."

"Nice to meet you," Elric said.

"The pleasures all mine," Raja replied. She was surprisingly polite, for a reptile.

"No offence, but you don't really look like a dragon," Lachlan piped up. "You look more like an overgrown lizard."

"I feel the same way," Raja said. "Though I am technically a dragon, for I am a komodo dragon, I'm nothing like the dragons everyone knows about, and it surprises me how many people take me for one. But then, the princes are all looking for an easy way to get the princess, and they probably think that I look enough like a dragon to qualify. But

I am much less dangerous and won't put up a fight. If it wasn't for Leilani here I would probably have been killed a long time ago."

"I don't help that much," Leilani said. "I always do the wrong thing."

"But it works regardless," Raja pointed out.

"If you don't mind my asking, how is it that you can speak?" Elric asked.

"Because I was not always a komodo dragon," Raja said. "I'm really a princess. It's really a pretty typical tale, wicked stepmother and all that, and I wanted to run away, but I couldn't. One day Leilani was flying past my window and accidentally propelled herself inside it when she sneezed–"

"Flying creates faerie dust," Leilani explained.

"I begged her to help me," Raja continued, undeterred, "asking her to turn me invisible so that I could escape. She refused because her magic always goes wrong. You see, whenever a faerie uses magic, it creates faerie dust, so it is only when she performs magic that she begins to sneeze, and when she sneezes the magic gets mixed up. I told her that anything would be better than being stuck with my wicked stepmother, and so she reluctantly agreed. It was actually going quite well, but the spell to turn one invisible is a long one, and at the very last moment she couldn't hold in the sneeze any longer and . . . well, you can see what happened."

"You poor thing!" Ada said.

"Oh, it's not so bad, really, other than the whole prince thing. When my stepmother saw me she near fainted away and I was able to leave without a fuss. I didn't really have anywhere to go, and neither did Leilani, so we've been exploring the forest for the past two months. It helps her, since she can ride me instead of flying everywhere."

"Flying is the hardest," Leilani said sadly. "It uses constant faerie dust."

"You've been roaming about for two

whole months?" Ada asked. "I was under the impression that all who are lost in any forest find Grandmother's House quite swiftly. It's the place where anyone is welcome, especially those running away."

"Then perhaps they weren't lost," Pem said.

"Where are you all going?" Raja asked.

"The faerie queen is in trouble and we're going to help her," Lachlan said.

"The faerie queen!" Raja and Leilani cried together.

"That's terrible!" Leilani said. "What happened to her?"

"We're not sure, but she needs help, and we're going to do all we can to help her," Ada said.

"Can we join you?" Raja asked.

"Yes, can we?" Leilani echoed.

"Certainly," Pem said. "The more help the better."

"Hey, that's not what you said when we asked!" Lachlan said.

"They don't have anyone expecting them home," Pem said. "Perhaps this is why they weren't lost. Perhaps they were searching for this journey."

That settled the whole situation. Raja offered to carry some of the baggage, and they soon set off through the woods.

The journey continued much in the same way it had up to this point. Ada and Elric were quite pleased at the new company, for it gave Lachlan a distraction. Instead of constantly talking to them or asking how much longer the journey was, he talked to Raja, who for one didn't seem to mind his enthusiasm. She actually seemed to be happy for the chance to make conversation.

"Do you think if we rescued the faerie queen that she could change you back?" Lachlan asked her.

"No, I don't think so," Raja said. "Faerie magic doesn't work on other faerie magic, and even the queen would be bound by rules such as that."

"Then what makes her different from the other faeries?"

"She has more powerful magic than the rest, and is in charge of all the faeries. But only the faerie who created the magic can do anything to it. In other words, Leilani is the only one who can change me back, but she's too afraid to try. Of course, if it was based on a stipulation, then fulfilling the stipulation would work, too, but Leilani didn't put any on me."

"So you're stuck like that forever?"

"Unless Leilani figures out how to control her magic, or changes me into something else."

"What's it like, being a dragon?" Lachlan asked.

"It takes some getting used to, being on all fours and all, but I actually almost enjoy it," Raja said. "I was getting a little tired of the whole princess expectation, always having to wear a nice dress and make sure my hair was exactly perfect and have the best manners while eating. As a dragon, I don't have to impress anyone, I don't have any hair, and I can eat as messily as I want to – which is good, because you can't really eat politely when you're a dragon. I can run rather fast in spurts, and I can climb trees, though it can be a bit difficult due to the added weight. But overall I have no responsibilities except finding food. Really the only downfall is those dratted princes."

"Are there really that many princes who find you?"

"Oh, you'd be surprised," Raja said with a sigh. "I've lost count of them by now, and it's only been two months since I changed into a dragon."

"What happened to them all?" Lachlan asked. "Did they all become frogs?"

"No, it was different each time, depending on how Leilani's magic backfired. One shrunk to the size of a pea, one simply lost his memory and walked away in confusion, and one even started proclaiming his vast love for me. That was rather awkward. It was all we could do to lose him. But anyway, you get the idea."

"Is it always princes? I would expect a few knights in shining armor to be mixed in there sometimes."

"I had thought as much myself, but never once did a knight come. I finally realized something: shining armor cannot remain shiny once it's been in a battle. Therefore, the knights in shining armor would no longer be just those if they actually tried to slay dragons. When I was a princess I'd always dreamed of one coming to rescue me from my wicked stepmother, but now I see why none ever came – and now I wouldn't want one anyway. I'd rather have a knight in tarnished armor. I mean, who wants a knight who hasn't gone out and lived up to his title by actually taking the risk of getting some dirt on his armor?"

"I never thought of it that way before," Lachlan said. "But on the other hand, even the knights in tarnished armor would have started with their armor shining."

"Good point," Raja replied. "I guess

you could say that the knights worth wanting are the ones who don't keep their armor shiny for long."

They talked for the rest of the day until Pem called it a night and everyone settled down to make camp.

"Are we getting close?" Elric asked Pem.

"Well, we're certainly getting closer, but we still have a ways to go," he answered. "But we are getting close enough that it won't be so easy from now on. Strange magic is up ahead. I can feel it, and I don't like it. It must have something to do with the trouble that the faerie queen is in. I suppose we'll find out pretty soon just what is to be expected."

Chapter Four

The House of Mirrors

The change was gradual, almost unnoticeable. It wasn't until the whole group had to detour around a large tree that Elric realized they had been sidestepping trees for some time now. As he thought about it, it occurred to him that the atmosphere itself simply didn't feel as safe as it had before. All the same, it wasn't a drastic difference, and nothing else hindered their progress or caused them any danger. It was more like the forest had been helping them before, but was now letting them pass without a bit of assistance.

On the fourth morning, they came to the end of the food that Grandmother had sent with them. When it came time for lunch, Raja set off into the woods to hunt and brought back a good size deer, which Ada cooked and served. Raja kept a piece of raw meat for herself and ate it behind a tree, for she had succumbed to a komodo dragon's diet.

When they were finished eating, the group halfheartedly pressed forward. They had been traveling for three and a half days, and now they were sore, tired, and bored. There had been some excitement when initiating the journey, but it was lost now in the monotony. It wasn't until rather late in the afternoon that something unusual happened, something that sparked everyone's interest instantly. There, in the middle of the wood, completely secluded from everything else, was a lone, dilapidated cottage. Wondering why there was a cottage so far from civilization, and hoping for some rest and food, they made for its door in an instant.

"Perhaps we shouldn't all clamber up

at once," Ada called out. "Who knows what sort of creature might live here. It could bring us all trouble if we're not careful. We should send just one person to scout it out."

Reluctantly, everyone agreed that she was right. They chose Leilani, as she was small enough to get in with the possibility of not being noticed. She squeezed through a crack in the wall and disappeared into the house while the rest waited breathlessly just behind the line of trees around it. It was only a moment before she returned.

"There doesn't seem to be anyone in here, but it's the strangest house I've ever seen! Come, see for yourselves!" she called.

They didn't need a second invitation. Lachlan was the first through the door.

"What . . . ?" he trailed off as he looked around the strange house.

"My, this is peculiar," Pem agreed. Everyone filed in and looked about, trying to make sense of the house before them. The furniture and walls were covered in dust and cobwebs, but only for a few feet, at which point the room was clean and put in order, full of all sorts of fancy things. Lachlan approached the clean side of the room, but when he came to the line that separated it he bumped into an invisible wall and could go no further.

"That's strange," he said. "I wonder what the other rooms are like." He turned and entered the door on the left side of the room they were in and found the same phenomena, though it was around a corner. Once again, he couldn't pass an invisible wall to the clean half of the room. There was another door at the other end of that room around another corner, and he went through that one, followed by the rest of the group, only to find a room much the same.

"It seems as though this house has four rooms that go in a square around the blocked off room in the middle," Raja observed.

"But that room in the middle seems to be much too big," Elric pointed out. "And shouldn't we be able to see the dilapidated room on the other side of it, if the wall is invisible all around it? But each room we've been into shows the middle room to have solid walls on all the other three sides."

"Elric's right," Ada said. "Something else is going on."

"It's like a mirror," Meleen said. It was the first thing she had said the entire trip.

"What was that?" Pem asked.

Meleen's cheeks turned red. "I just meant that in every room we've been in, the middle room has the same furniture and set up, only it's clean on that side and dirty over here. There's even a picture that's the same, see?"

She pointed to a portrait of a beautiful woman hanging on the wall opposite the middle room that was covered in dust and tilted at an odd angle, while on the wall of the clean room was the same picture, spotless and perfectly straight.

"It is a mirror!" Lachlan cried. "See, the woman is facing the opposite direction on that side!"

"But why would the reflection be different than the actual room?" Ada asked.

"And why aren't we in the reflection?" Elric said.

"What are you doing in my house?" a shrill voice demanded in rage. To their surprise, a woman who looked very similar to the one in the portrait had just entered the room from the one room they hadn't checked yet, only she didn't come into the same room they were in, but rather into the reflection of the room. Everyone was too shocked and confused to answer.

"How did you find this place?" the woman continued. "What do you want with–" she broke off, her eyes widening as she spotted a member of the group she hadn't seen before. "What is that *thing?!*"

"What? Where?" Pem cried, looking about for some monster or something.

"It's called a komodo dragon," Elric said. "But you don't have to worry, we mean you no harm."

"That doesn't really look like a dragon to me," the woman said, her brow drawing down.

"That's what I said!" Lachlan replied.

"Would you mind explaining this house?" Ada asked. "I've never seen anything like it."

"Yes, it once was the most spectacular house, as you can see from the reflection," the woman said bitterly.

"So it is a reflection," Lachlan said. Ada shushed him.

"As you can also undoubtedly see, I am the most beautiful woman in the world," the woman continued, pretending not to hear the interruption. "I had this cottage built specifically for my taste, designed so that it went in a square around one large mirror in the middle, so that I could see myself no matter where I was in the house. I built it just outside of a village so that it wouldn't be associated with the other common houses, but would still be close enough that I could journey into the village whenever I wished to grace the villagers with the pleasure of seeing my beauty.

"And then, one day, it was all ruined. This self-absorbed faerie happened upon my house. She was the strangest faerie I'd ever seen, for she had a tail."

"A tail!" Pem exclaimed. "Do you realize who that was?"

"No, she didn't introduce herself, but I told her how unfashionable her tail was, and she twirled her arm in the air, and the next thing I knew I was trapped on the wrong side of the mirror! Not only that, but through the window I could see that she moved the house away from the village so that no one could see me. Luckily, as the mirror goes around the whole house, I still have access to it all, but I simply can't leave."

"That's harsh," Elric said.

"It serves you right, if I do say so myself," Leilani said with a scowl, "insulting the faerie queen like that."

"Wait, that was the faerie queen?" Elric

asked. "Are you sure?"

"Yes, of course it was," Pem said. "The faerie queen is distinguished from the other faeries by her tail. She is the only faerie privileged to have one."

"Unfortunately," Ada said, "most people don't understand what a great honor this is among the faeries. In fact, this is what caused me to be so tall. The faerie queen herself came to my birth to place a faerie gift on me, but my parents laughed at her for looking so unusual. She told them that she had been planning to bless their daughter, but now that they had judged her appearance, she would curse them to have the same problem by causing me to grow so tall that they would be disgraced in all Malmor, for all Malmor looked at appearances."

"Well, you're in luck," Pem said to the woman. "We are currently on a journey to save this very faerie, the only one who can change you back, from an unknown terror. When we succeed, we can mention you to her, and perhaps she will be generous enough to free you from the curse she placed upon you."

"Oh, yes, that would be great," she replied. "It would certainly be wonderful to get out of this reflection."

"What name should I give her?" Pem asked.

"Superbia," the woman replied. "Surely you've heard of me."

No one had.

"Well then, Superbia, I will do my best to revert you back to your original state," Pem promised. "We had best be on our way to ensure our hasty recovery of the faerie queen."

"Wait, can I ask for one more favor?" Superbia asked.

"Of course, what is it?" Pem answered.

"You see, though being in this mirror has the advantage of never aging, and thus preserving my beauty for all these long years, it also has the most horrid downfall: since I'm trapped in the mirror, I have no way to see my own reflection! I haven't seen myself in ages. Would any of you by chance have a mirror that you could hold up so that I could see myself once again, just for a moment?"

And she called the faerie queen self-absorbed! Elric thought.

"Yes, actually, I believe I packed a handheld mirror in my bags," Ada said. "If you'll wait a moment while I find it..." She began to shuffle through one of her bags. "Ah, here it is. Is this good?"

"Turn it a little to the left... a little higher..." Superbia tried to adjust herself as well to get a view of herself the little mirror. "I do believe it's too dim to see anything. Could you hold it more by the window, at an angle so that it catches the setting light?" Ada did as requested, but just as the light reflected from the handheld mirror to Superbia's face, the entire wall mirror lit up brilliantly. It only lasted for a moment, but when Ada moved the mirror in surprise out of the sunlight, all were astonished to find the wall mirror to be just that, a normal mirror. No longer was the reflection unchanged by the effects of the years; no longer did Superbia stand there. Now it reflected the room as it was, with the group staring at themselves, who stared back.

"What happened to her?" Elric asked.

"Where am I? What's going on?" Superbia's voice cried.

Ada turned the mirror in her hands over and saw what she suspected: Superbia had somehow been transferred from the wall mirror to the handheld one, and now the mirror in Ada's hands didn't reflect as it should, but revealed Superbia's face.

"Well, that was unexpected," Pem said.

"I suppose we'll have to take her along then," Elric said.

Ada eyed the bag that the mirror had come out of hesitantly. Since the mirror was still facing her, Superbia saw the look.

"Don't even think about stuffing me in that bag," she sneered. "The least you can do after getting me into this mess is carry me properly."

After a few faulty experiments, they finally settled on sticking the mirror's handle into Elric's belt, with the glass facing out so Superbia could see. After that, there wasn't much to do except leave. All the food had long since spoiled, so they weren't able to procure any of it, much to everyone's dismay. They considered spending the night there, ignoring Superbia's protests, but in the end they determined it was too dusty to get a good night's sleep. They didn't go very far before settling down in the grass for the night.

The next day Elric could see an even greater difference in the woods. Now they were constantly forced to detour around large trees, and there never seemed to be enough room between them. More than once he hit his head even though he kept watch for low branches. Even as clumsy as he was, he had never bumped into so many things in his life. Everyone was getting frustrated, even Bia, as they had begun to call her, who kept shouting at Elric to be more careful, claiming many times that she nearly got scratched by a branch. The only one who seemed undeterred was Pem, who encouraged everyone heartily to press on, declaring that this was a great sign, for it meant that they were getting close.

To make matters worse, they began hearing sounds of frightening animals. There had always been animals rustling about in the trees, but those were harmless things like birds and squirrels. Now they heard snarls and growls, and the birds were less and less frequent. Raja seemed to be the most fearful, as she could smell the animals all around.

The real danger began when Ada cried out in pain.

"What happened?" Elric asked.

"One of the branches scratched me," she said, looking over a fresh cut on her arm. "If I didn't know better, I could have sworn that branch lurched out at me."

Elric took a good look at the scratch while Meleen found some ointment and cloths they had packed and began dressing it.

"It doesn't look very deep," Elric assured his wife. "It should heal pretty quickly."

"What's wrong, Raja?" Lachlan asked, noticing that she had stiffened.

"The blood," she said. "They smell it."

"Do you think they're going to attack us?" Lachlan asked, wide-eyed.

"I don't know, but it certainly got their attention," Raja said. They waited uncertainly for a moment while Raja flicked her tongue out several times, turning her head this way and that.

"They're starting to come toward us," she said.

"What are we going to do?" Ada said.

"The trees," Lachlan said. "If we climb them, maybe we can get out of their reach."

They didn't hesitate. Raja climbed one

tree rather easily and helped Lachlan and Meleen up while Ada struggled up another. The trees seemed to be downright revolting and they nearly fell out several times as they got settled in. Pem somehow wound up very high up in another tree, sitting quietly with plenty of room on his branch, even though there didn't seem to be enough branches below him to have let him climb up. Ada looked down and saw Elric still on the ground staring up uncertainly.

"Elric!" she cried. "You have to get up here! Surely your fear of heights isn't greater than your fear of getting attacked by these wild animals!"

"I . . . I just . . ." Elric stammered.

"Come on, I'll help you," Ada said. "Just don't look down."

She readjusted herself and reached down to him. He hesitated, then grasped her outstretched hand and clamored up the tree to sit beside her. He rested his head against the trunk of the tree, his eyes closed and his breath laborious. He made it just in time, for no sooner had he sat down than a pack of wolves sprang through the trees beneath them, followed soon by a bear and two tigers. They were all angered to find their prey to be beyond their reach, but in their rage they ended up turning on each of the other types of animals.

Eventually they gave up and dispersed. Even still, Raja cautioned them to wait for few minutes until they were quite far out of the area. While they were waiting anxiously, Elric shifted, despising the predicament. Unfortunately, in his distress it did not occur to him that the side that Bia was on was the one beside the trunk, and as he shifted the mirror bumped against the trunk and came loose from his belt. With a shriek Bia fell to the ground below.

"Bia!" Ada cried.

"I . . . I think I'm alright," Bia called back. "I don't seem to be broken."

Ada started to try to climb down, but Raja said, "Not yet, there's something else coming. If Bia survived the fall, then she should be ignored by whatever it is."

"You're going to leave me here?" Bia wailed. They didn't have time to answer, for just then a fox appeared.

"A fox?" Lachlan said. "You think that's too dangerous to face?"

"I wasn't sure what it was," Raja said, a bit embarrassed. The fox looked up when it heard their voices but ignored them and sniffed around the ground. Raja was wrong; it went almost straight to Bia. Before anyone could react, it snatched the mirror by the handle in its mouth and ran off into the trees.

"Ahhh!" Bia cried. "Help!"

Unfortunately, by the time Raja and Pem climbed down, the first two to reach the ground, Raja declared that she was too far gone, for the fox was very fast. With nothing else to do about it, they helped the others get down from the trees and decided that they really should be moving on, hoping to come to the end of the forest as fast as possible.

Chapter Five

Kron

The fox knew its way around the forest well, and around sunset, Bia, who had long since given up protesting, saw that they were leaving the wood and approaching a large castle, for she was being carried sideways so that she faced forward. Surrounding the castle was a great multitude of knights in armor, but they were stock-still and let the fox pass without resistance. In fact, they were so still that Bia wondered if they were just empty armor placed around for intimidation.

The fox carried Bia through a small swinging door built into the front door, obviously designed specifically for the fox to pass through, and along the hall until the fox stopped at a door, though how it knew which one was the right one in the vast quantity of doors along the hall was beyond her.

The fox eased her down on the ground and yipped twice. The door opened and a man looked down.

"Why, hello, Twain," the man said. "What have you brought me this time? A mirror?" He bent down and picked up the mirror, then gasped. "Oh, my! This is incredible! A magic mirror! Thank you very much, Twain."

"Wait, what? I'm not–" Bia sputtered, but then realized that it could be to her advantage to have him believe her to be a magic mirror. The man hadn't really heard her as he closed the door and hurried over to a sit on a couch in the room.

"Oh, Magic Mirror," he said to Bia, "I am extremely honored to be in possession of you, you have no idea. My name is Kron. It's so nice to finally have someone to talk to. Miriam is always off on her own business and the other faerie doesn't like to talk much, and she doesn't seem to like me anyway. I can only talk to Twain, but foxes can't talk, as I'm sure you know, so he's not much of a conversationalist. That is, you do talk, don't you?"

"Of course I do!" Bia said.

"Beg pardon, I didn't mean to offend," Kron said. "I just know very little about magic mirrors, though I suppose all magic mirrors I've heard of can talk. I mean, after all, that's what makes them magic mirrors, right? What other things can you do? Can you show me someone I want to see?"

"Well, I . . ."

"Actually, there isn't anyone I want to see, so never mind," he said, saving her. "What else? Maybe you know details about things, like who is the fairest in the land."

"Why, I–"

"Except that I don't actually care about who is the fairest in the land," Kron cut her off before she said that she was the fairest. "Actually, there really isn't anyone in the land anyway, except for the wild animals and Twain and the two faeries. At least, not that I know of. Oh! I know! Are you in good standing with faeries?"

"That depends," Bia said. "What did you have in mind?"

"You see, I have a dilemma. You probably can't tell, since you're a mirror, but I'm actually a midget. I felt like an outcast in the land I was from, so I ran away. In the woods I found a faerie named Miriam, and I asked her to help me. She said that she herself couldn't do anything to help, but that she knew of a faerie that could, a faerie that had once made a girl grow very tall. She brought me to this castle that was the perfect size for me and told me how to get this faerie to come.

"I followed her instructions and sure enough the faerie came. But when I made my request, she refused to do it. Miriam, disappointed that I hadn't been helped, made the faerie stay until she agreed to do so, but ever since then the faerie hasn't spoken at all. I don't see why she doesn't want to help me. She of all faeries should know how hard it is to be different from everyone else since she's the only faerie I've ever heard of who has a tail."

"She has a tail?" Bia asked. "Are you sure?"

"Very sure," Kron said. "That was how Miriam told me I would be able to identify her. Anyway, I was wondering if maybe I could bring you to her and you could convince her to make me bigger. I figure that magic mirrors would have some influence with faeries. Do you?"

"I would be willing to try," Bia said, though she didn't actually have any intention of doing so. She knew that this could be her ticket out.

"Wonderful!" Kron said. "I'll never forget this."

He proceeded at once to take her to the room in which the faerie was being kept, babbling the whole time about how delighted he was that she was helping him. When they entered the room, he held Bia up so that she could see the occupant. The small faerie with a long tail, the very one that had cursed Bia to her confinement, sat facing the wall away from the door. Bia saw that there was a semi transparent ball surrounding her.

"Faerie," Kron called to her, "have you changed your mind yet?"

The faerie didn't answer.

"Then perhaps my mirror can talk some sense into you," he said.

This got her attention, and she turned to see what he was talking about.

"Remember me?" Bia said.

"Oh, my," the faerie said. "How did you get into there? I left you in a full-length mirror."

"Yes, that's right," Bia sneered. "You left me in that cursed mirror in the middle of the woods with nothing to do for years. I was stuck in that moment, unable to sleep, unable to leave, unable to show my beauty. And now I'm stuck in this contraption."

"Wait, you mean you're not actually a magic mirror?" Kron asked.

The faerie giggled. "Magic mirror? What a ridiculous notion. There's no such thing as magic mirrors. They're only myths! No, this is just a prideful woman who needed a lesson – and doesn't seem to have learned it yet."

"What's that supposed to mean?" Bia demanded.

"You have to figure it out for yourself," she said. "When you do, you'll be changed back."

"That's not fair!" Bia cried. "You can't even tell me what I have to do?"

"If I did, you would never get out of the mirror, for you would just be pretending," she replied.

Bia didn't really understand what that meant, but she tried to figure out another way to convince her. "What if we freed you. Would you do it as a reward?"

"What?" Kron exclaimed. "But she's only stuck here until she makes me taller!"

"Is that what she told you?" the faerie asked.

"What do you mean?" Kron said.

"Miriam was just using you to lure me here," she answered. "She's always coveted my position as queen of the faeries, but was never able to do anything about it. So she got you to trick me into falling into her trap, and now she has me locked in a magic cage. Even if I agreed to make you grow, I couldn't because my magic wouldn't be able to get past her magic cage."

"I don't see a magic cage," Kron said.

"It's that ball around her," Bia said.

"What ball? There's nothing around her."

"Interesting," the faerie noted. "Miriam must have made the cage invisible to humans so that you wouldn't realize just how I was trapped, but mirrors often reflect things the way they really are, rather than the way they appear to be, so she must be able to see what a mirror reflects."

"So if we got you out of the cage, would you change me back?" Bia pressed.

The faerie considered it. "It is true, whoever helps a faerie in need must be rewarded with a faerie gift of the rescuer's request. I still think it would be better for you to change back by learning your lesson, but I really must get out before Miriam does something drastic, so yes, if you can free me I'll do as you ask. But there are only two ways I know of getting free, and neither one is easy."

"What are they?" Bia asked.

"There is a man who would be able to help me," the faerie replied. "I called for his help, but it's been several days. If you can find him and bring him here, then he will be able to release me."

"I think he may already be on his way," Bia said. "I was traveling with a group of people and a creature and a faerie, all who were coming with the intent to save you."

"That is good news indeed," the faerie

said. "If Pem is on his way, then there is hope after all!"

"But I don't know how he can get inside," Kron stated. "There are guards all about the castle."

"Wait, I thought you said that there weren't any other humans in the land," Bia said.

"Oh, they're not human," Kron said. "They're armor. Miriam enchanted them to come alive so that they could guard the castle. Quite clever, really, for they can never be defeated."

"Pem might be able to get past them still," the faerie said. "How many are there?"

"Too many to count," Kron replied.

"Hmm, then it might be too many," she replied. "With Pem, it's hard to know."

"If we can't get Pem here, then what is the other way to free you?" Bia asked.

"Miriam," the faerie said. "She's the only faerie who can take back the magic she bestowed. But that would be extremely difficult, for I can't imagine her actually releasing the magic of her own accord, and the only other way her magic could be broken is if she was dead, and that would be very difficult to accomplish, as well. I'd say your best chance is to find a way to bring Pem into the castle. But you must be cautious about it. If Miriam discovers that you plan to release me, she will turn against you relentlessly. She may even suspect Pem's arrival and be planning a trap for him as well."

"We'll do what we can," Bia said.

"And if we succeed, will you also make me taller?" Kron asked.

"If that is what you wish," the faerie said.

"Then you have my word, I will try with all my ability to see to your freedom," Kron promised.

Chapter Six

The Stone Prince

The next day the group arrived at the end of the forest. It had been a terrible day, after a restless night without much sleep, and everyone was relieved – that is, until they saw the vast guard that awaited them.

"Now what do we do?" Lachlan groaned. "We'll never get past those guards.

"That's strange," Raja said, flicking out her tongue again.

"What?" Elric asked.

"I don't smell any humans in all that armor," she said. "They just smell like metal. Inside the castle there's one human, and . . . wait, the fox is in there!

And he's coming this way!"

Sure enough, the fox came trotting out of the castle and headed directly toward the group that was still mostly hidden behind the trees. It carried something in its mouth and dropped it on the ground in front of Pem. He picked it up and declared that it was a rolled up piece of paper. Opening it, he read the message aloud.

"'The faerie queen is trapped in a ball of magic by a wicked faerie and can't get out. We're trying to free her, but we need your help. Unfortunately, the guards are undefeatable enchanted armor, and we don't know how to get you into the castle. If you have any ideas, please send them back by way of the fox. Signed, Kron and Bia.'"

"Bia!" everyone chorused.

"Wow, I didn't think she actually cared about helping," Ada said.

"She's probably just doing it to get out of the mirror," Elric retorted.

"This is good," Pem said. "Now we

have someone inside the castle. The question is, how can they help us?"

"If they can get the other faerie to release the armor from the enchantment, then we can get into the castle," Leilani said.

"But if they could do that, then they could get the queen free," Lachlan said.

"Maybe they could cause a distraction to get the attention of the armor so that they leave a spot unmanned – so to speak," Raja said.

"Yes, yes, that could work." Pem turned the paper over and, once Ada found a pen among her belongings, wrote the suggestion on the back side, then rolled it up and handed it to the fox, who hurried back to the castle.

They waited a few moments until the fox came back with another message: "We'll try. It might take a while, though. Try to get to the back side of the castle, away from the woods, if you can."

After agreeing that there was enough space for them to get around the castle in a wide enough circle that the armor wouldn't see them, they sent the fox back with a message of consent. They followed the instructions, first journeying far to the right under the cover of the trees. Once they felt they were a good distance away, they left the woods and went into the open ground.

But they had only gone a few feet when the ground fell away and Elric found himself falling, or rather, sliding. Though thrown into confusion, part of his mind registered that they must have stepped into a trap. The slide lasted a moment, and he tumbled to a stop, coughing and sputtering as dust rose all around from his landing. He could hear others doing the same.

"Is everyone okay?" Ada cried.

"Yes," Elric said, "I am, at least."

"Me too," came Meleen's quiet voice. There were no more replies.

"What about everyone else?" Ada asked.

"I don't think there's anyone else down

here," Elric said as his eyes adjusted to the dim room. "We must have been the only three to fall through."

"Well, then at least they still have a chance," Ada said. "Where are we?"

"Probably in some dungeon or something," Elric said.

"Do you think there is a way out?" Ada asked.

They explored the room and found that it was small and completely enclosed except for the slide that had dropped them off, which was too steep for them to climb, and a hole in the ceiling that they determined was designed for ventilation. It was a rather high ceiling, and a rather small hole, but they realized it must have been made with shorter intruders in mind, for Elric could reach it.

"We could crawl through there and find our way out," Ada said.

"No, it's too small," Elric said. "I couldn't fit, and neither could you, though Meleen might."

"Meleen?" Ada asked. "Do you want to

try? You don't have to if you don't want to."

"I'll do it," she said. There was a strange determination in her voice they had never heard before. Elric lifted the girl up so she could reach the hole, and she pulled herself through. She followed the ventilation shaft until she reached another room and stuck her head through the hole. Though she could hardly see in the darkness, she made out what appeared to be a figure in the room.

"Hello?" she called. "Is someone in here?"

No reply. She debated whether to leave the small tunnel, since she probably wouldn't be able to reach it again, but she figured she would have to leave it at some point. It occurred to her that though it was dim in the room, there was still a little light. The scarce light from the other room had come from the tunnel they had fallen through, but where was this light coming from? She looked around for the source and saw that it came from a passageway leading out of the room. The room wasn't sealed! Perhaps this passage would lead somewhere.

She lowered herself down carefully as best she could, then dropped the rest of the way. She could just make out a lantern near the passageway entrance and set about trimming it. When it was lit, she turned back to the figure she had seen to find out what it was. She discovered that it was a statue of a handsome man. His right arm was outstretched and his eyes were wide, as though startled. He looked so realistic that Meleen half-expected him to start moving or speaking.

She wondered why a statue would have been made of a man in such a posture, and why it would be hidden away. It reminded her of something, a story she once heard, though she couldn't remember the exact details. Something about a person being turned into stone until someone changed them back. How were they changed back? Meleen wasn't sure, but it seemed like in all the stories it was a kiss that did the trick. A prince kissed a princess who was asleep and woke her, a prince kissed a princess who had died and revived her, and so on. Meleen found herself suddenly compelled to kiss the statue.

Her cheeks flushed as she realized how foolish that idea was. She didn't even know if it actually was a real person who had been changed to stone in the first place, and even if he was, how did she know a kiss would work? It occurred to her that in all the stories, it was as equally foolish for the princes to do what they did. In fact, they probably didn't even expect the princesses to wake up, so why were they going around kissing dead princesses?

On the other hand, what if he really was waiting for a kiss to wake him up, and Meleen just left him like that? Certainly it couldn't hurt for her to try. If he did turn into a human, then it would be wonderful, and if nothing happened, no one would ever know her foolishness.

Before she could talk herself out of it, and almost before she knew what she was doing, Meleen gave the statue a quick peck and stepped back to see if anything happened, her cheeks flushing again. Nothing. Disappointed, she began to turn away.

Clunk. It was so soft that she almost didn't hear it, but it was so quiet in the room that it caught her attention. It had come from the ground by the statue. Meleen turned back to see what it was. *Clunk. Cl-clunk. Clunk.* Pieces of rock hit the ground at the statues feet. Meleen raised her eyes and saw that they came from the statue, as pieces broke away, revealing human flesh. It had worked!

When the rock fell away from his eyes, the man blinked and looked around in surprise. The rock fell from his mouth, and he let out a choked startled sound. The rock started falling apart faster now, and it was only a few short moments before he was completely free, his right arm falling to his side.

"You, you saved me?" he asked. Meleen nodded, wide-eyed. The man was even more handsome as a human. "Why, then you must be my bride. Will you marry me?"

Meleen's jaw dropped at his forwardness.

"My apologies," the man said. "I see I was too hasty. I just assumed that whoever saved me would be my true love."

"It's just . . . we don't even know each other's names!" Meleen said.

"Oh, good point," he replied. "I am Prince Nolan, heir to this castle. What is your name?"

"Meleen," she answered.

"What a beautiful name," he said. "And you are just as beautiful. Lovely Meleen, will you consider being my bride, please?"

Somehow, even though it was such a sudden development, Meleen actually thought it sounded like a good idea. After all, in all of the stories with the kisses they ended up getting married right away. What did she think would happen otherwise?

Meleen gave a shy nod. "But I don't know if this is the best time. The faerie queen is being held captive in this castle by another faerie, and two of my friends are trapped in a room we fell into."

"Oh, I see. I bet the faerie queen was captured by the same dratted faerie that snuck into my castle and turned me into stone. I don't know how much I can do about that, but I can get your friends out. I know all of the passages under the castle, and I think I may know just the room you are speaking of."

Prince Nolan offered her his arm, and the two of them headed down the passageway.

Chapter Seven

Storming the Castle

em, Lachlan, Raja, and Leilani all watched in dismay as the other three fell through the ground ahead of them.

"It must be a trap!" Pem exclaimed. He peered down the opening and declared, "I do believe it is too deep for them to climb out."

"Uh, I hate to sound insensitive but . . . I don't think they're the only ones with a problem," Raja said.

"The guards!" Leilani said.

Looking up, Pem and Lachlan saw that some of the guards had noticed what had happened and were running toward them, swords raised. Pem, Lachlan, and

Raja, with Leilani still sitting on her back, turned and ran back into the woods, but one of the guards who had made it the farthest pressed through the woods after them. Pem, who was in the back of the group, tripped on a root and sprawled on the ground.

"Pem!" the others shouted.

The guard who had been trailing them tripped on the same root and fell in a heap on top of Pem.

"Oof!" Pem grunted under the load.

Lachlan ran back towards them with every intention of fending off the armor, and pushed it off Pem only to realize that it had stopped moving. It was as lifeless as any normal piece of armor.

"What happened to it?" Lachlan asked.

"Well, I supposed I must have dispelled the faerie magic that kept it alive when it touched me," Pem said.

"What are you talking about?" Lachlan said.

"I can dispel faerie magic by touching it," Pem said, as though it were obvious.

"What! Why didn't you tell us this a long time ago?" Raja said. "You mean this whole time you could have changed me and Bia back to our rightful states, and stopped all of those guards just by touching them?!"

"Oh, heaven's no!" Pem said. "I could never change anyone back. What do you think I am?"

Lachlan, Raja, and Leilani began to wonder just what indeed they thought he was, but none ventured to say so.

"No, no, if I had touched either you or Bia it would have been disastrous. As for the guards, you don't actually mean you expect me to run into the midst of all those sharp swords and hope that I can deactivate them before they run me through, do you?"

"Sorry," Raja said. "It's just so unexpected. It would have been nice to know going into this."

"Then I apologize as well," Pem said. "I hadn't realized it was so important."

"Maybe we can still use this," Lachlan

said. "When the distraction comes, you can go first in case any of the guards lag behind and see us. Oh! I have a brilliant idea! The armor looks about my size; I can put it on now that it's lifeless for extra protection."

"Yes, that is a good idea," Pem said, and he began to help Lachlan strap on the armor. No sooner had they finished than a tumult erupted far to their left.

"That must be the distraction," Raja said.

They stepped out of the forest to see and found that many of the wild animals had emerged from the woods, causing the guards to all head over to them.

"We need to go now, before the battle is over," she continued. "We must be quick."

"Um, I just realized a problem with the armor," Lachlan said after a few steps. "It's too heavy. I can't run very fast at all!"

"Here, get on my back and I'll carry you," Raja suggested.

"Are you sure you can manage?" Lachlan asked.

"Yes, I'm surprisingly strong in this body," Raja said.

Without an argument Lachlan climbed onto her back, and Raja and Pem set off toward the castle. As Lachlan had anticipated, several of the guards had lagged back and now turned their attention to them.

Pem focused on those to the left, dodging their swipes and touching each set of armor however he managed to, at which point they would topple over, while Lachlan focused on those on the right, knocking them back with his sword and blocking their attacks with his armor. Raja helped him as best she could, swatting at them with her powerful tail and hitting them with her claws, but she couldn't do much for fear of knocking Lachlan off her back. It was going quite well until a guard landed a strike on Lachlan and sent him flying off Raja. Pem turned and slapped the guard's arm, causing it to crash to the ground.

"Lachlan!" Raja cried and hurried to his side.

He sat up dazedly. "Is my armor tarnished enough now?" he said with a chuckle.

Raja smiled in relief, her dragon teeth gleaming in the sun.

"I think I'm too tired to keep this up," Lachlan continued.

Raja couldn't answer, for guards had reached them and she did her best to keep them at bay, though Leilani hopped off of her head and stayed by Lachlan.

"Leilani, I have an idea," he said. "If that faerie can animate armor, why can't we? You're a faerie, you can do it, too!"

"That blow must have knocked the sense out of you," Leilani cried in disbelief. "You know I never get my magic right! I always sneeze and mess it up."

"Have you ever tried holding your nose so that you don't breath in the dust?" Lachlan suggested.

The faerie hesitated. "No, actually, I never thought of that."

"Then there's no better time than now to try!" Lachlan said.

Leilani took a deep breath, said, "Don't be surprised if it turns you into a duck," plugged her nose with one hand, and twirled her other arm in the air. There was a flash, and then nothing. Leilani let go of her nose and sneezed. "Did it work?

"I'm not sure," Lachlan said, "but at least I didn't – whooooooooaaaaa!"

He suddenly found himself getting up and standing involuntarily. He was forced to face Leilani and salute.

"It worked! I didn't make it do that! You did it, Leilani!"

"I . . . I did? I did!" she exclaimed.

"Um, I think it's waiting for your instructions," Lachlan said when he tried to get the armor to move, but to no avail.

"Oh, yes, of course," Leilani said. "Ahem. Armor, you are to fight against the other armor, and you are to listen to the orders of the boy inside you."

The armor nodded, conking Lachlan on the head, earning an "Ouch!" from him. Then it set about attacking the other guards, taking Lachlan along for the ride. It was quite a strange experience, being moved without trying to.

"Armor," Lachlan called, "head to the wall as you fight." The armor obeyed and began working its way to the wall, beside Raja and Pem. It wasn't long before they reached it. "Wait, how are we going to get inside?"

"I can climb the wall," Raja said. "Get on my back again. Pem, you can get on, too."

"No, don't you remember? I can't touch you! But it doesn't matter, I'm sure I can find my way up the wall myself."

Lachlan ordered the armor to let him be in control, and sat down on Raja, but she didn't make it up the wall very far.

"I'm sorry, you're too heavy in that armor," she apologized as she returned to the ground.

"I'll take it off and let it fight on its

own," Lachlan said. Though more of the guards were coming back from the distraction, for most of the animals had been defeated, Pem and Raja were able to keep them away as Lachlan freed himself from the armor. Once he did, he ordered the armor to go back to fighting the others, and settled once again on Raja's back.

She began scrambling up the wall, going much more easily now that the added weight was lost. But it was tiring duty, and as she neared the top she feared she wouldn't be able to make it. She had almost reached it when she started to slip back and cried out. Pem, who had somehow gotten up before them, saw their predicament and lunged forward, grabbing her arm and pulling her over the top of the wall. When they were safely on the ground, Lachlan tumbled off her back.

"Good job, Raja!" he said.

She hissed, then started back, surprised at herself.

"Oh! Oh, no!" Pem cried. "Raja, I'm so sorry, I wasn't thinking! This is terrible!"

"What happened?" Lachlan asked. "Pem, what happens when you touch something that has been changed into something else?"

"Transformation magic is a tricky kind, you see," Pem said, his voice filled with regret. "It's different from the other magic. When someone gets changed into something else, they retain some faerie magic, which is what enables them to retain their speech, and a faerie can change them back by reversing the magic. But I dispel the magic, meaning . . ."

"Meaning, she's now a full komodo dragon?" Lachlan guessed.

"Exactly," Pem said.

"That's not so bad," Lachlan said. "Now the faerie queen herself can change her back! Actually, it's better this way, because now Leilani doesn't have to worry about doing it, even though she learned how to control her magic."

"I'm afraid it's not that simple," Pem

said. "There's something else about transformation magic. If something gets transformed, and then changes back, there is no problem. They can go on changing into various things the rest of their lives as long as they always change back. But . . . if the magic is dispelled while they were in the other form, then . . . they're stuck in that form. Forever. No amount of faerie magic can change them after that. I'm sorry."

Lachlan looked at Raja. So she was to be a dragon for the rest of her life. And now she couldn't even talk. She met his gaze, her eyes pinched with sadness. Finally, her dismay turned into determination and she jerked her head toward the end of the passageway they had climbed into.

"You're right," Lachlan agreed. "We've come this far, we need to finish this."

Chapter Eight

A Turn of Events

Kron had sent Twain into the woods to rile up all the animals it could find to come distract the guards. He watched the progress through a window overlooking the whole yard on that side, holding Bia up to see it as well. Now that he knew she was a real person, not a magic mirror, he had been less domineering of the conversation, though he still was quite a bit, and they had talked for a long time while they had waited for the others to arrive. Bia hadn't been used to listening to other people, but to her surprise she realized that she actually rather enjoyed it. Now they watched the battle together and chatted until they spotted the disruption to their left.

"Look! They're breaking through!" Kron pointed to group as they made their way up the wall.

"Why is the knight riding on the princess's back?" Bia asked.

"What are you talking about?" Kron asked. "He's riding an overgrown lizard."

"Wait, you mean *she's* the dragon they were talking about? Then what is that funny looking man?"

"There's no funny looking man," Kron said. "Just a knight and a dragon and a normal man."

"You call rabbit ears and a horse tail normal?" Bia asked. But before Kron could respond they were interrupted by a shrill cry.

"I suppose *you* are the cause of this!"

Kron whirled around to find Miriam fuming as she hovered in the entrance to the room.

"What is this all about?" she demanded. "What do you mean by attacking my guards?

You know they're indestructible."

"Perhaps you have some explaining of your own to do," Kron countered. "What exactly do you mean to do with that faerie you trapped? You told me she would make me taller, but you didn't really expect her to do that, did you?"

"Oh, you and your wish to be tall!" Miriam cried. "As if that's all that mattered! I tell you, there are many more important things than *that!* You think you're so small; I'll show you small!"

She began twirling her arm in the air.

"Kron, hold me up in front of you!" Bia cried, realizing what was happening.

"But you'll be destroyed!"

"I know, but I . . . I don't care! Do it anyway!" she yelled. Kron obeyed just as Miriam sent a blast of magic toward him. There was a flash and Kron felt himself knocked down, though not by magic. Something crashed into him. When the flash cleared, he found it was a woman that had fallen against him, and that the mirror was shattered into pieces.

"Oh! Oh, my," the woman said.

"Bia! You're out of the mirror!" he exclaimed.

"Yes, I am, aren't I?" she replied, still a bit dazed.

"But how? I thought that would be the death of you!"

"So did I," she said. "Maybe that's what did it. In that moment, I cared for your safety more than mine. Maybe that's what it took to break the curse, caring about someone else more than myself."

"What!" Miriam shrieked. "What happened to me?"

Kron and Bia turned to see what was going on, but they couldn't find her.

"Where is she?" Kron asked.

"Look, there!" Bia cried, pointing. On the floor below where Miriam had been flying was a small ant. "When the blast hit the mirror it must have reflected back to her and changed her into the very thing she was going to change you into!"

The ant lifted its front right arm and began twirling it in the air. Though both

Kron and Bia knew what that signified, they couldn't stop themselves from laughing. You would, too, if you saw an ant twirling its arm in the air. It's quite comical, to be sure.

Just then, Lachlan burst into the room. He didn't see the tiny ant on the ground, but she saw him. In fact, his foot was the last thing she ever saw.

"Bia!" he cried when he saw her.

"In the flesh!" she answered.

"Congratulations," he said. "But where is the wicked faerie you mentioned?"

"I believe she's on the bottom of your shoe," Kron said.

Lachlan checked. Sure enough, there was a smudge on his shoe that had once been the ant, that had once been the faerie.

"You did it, Lachlan!" Pem arrived after him along with Raja and Leilani. "You defeated her! Look at the armor!" Everyone peered out the window and saw all of the armor falling to the ground. All except for one, of course.

"The faerie queen!" Kron remembered. "She'll be free now! Come, follow me, I'll take you to her."

As they all headed toward the room the queen had been kept in, Kron realized something.

"Bia, you're shorter than me!" he said.

"Oh, yes, I suppose I am," she said.

"And that boy is, too!" Kron further declared.

"How tall are you, exactly?" Bia asked.

"Five-foot-six," Kron answered.

"Why, that's not short at all!" Bia said. "Where I'm from, that's actually quite tall!"

"You must be from the land Elric is from," Lachlan said. "Everyone there is about nine feet tall, but everyone in my homeland is closer to five feet."

"You mean all this time there's been a land of midgets?" Kron cried.

"We're not midgets," Lachlan protested. "The others are just giants!"

"Yes," Bia answered. "There's a land full of people you would fit right in with."

"That's wonderful!"

They turned a corner and found Elric, Ada, Meleen, a stranger, and the faerie queen.

"You guys are alright!" Pem cried.

"Pem!" the faerie queen said. "I'm so happy to see you!"

"Gloriana!" Pem said in return. "I'm so happy to see that you are safe!"

"How did you defeat Miriam?" the faerie queen asked him.

"I didn't," he replied. "Lachlan did."

Everyone turned to the boy in surprise.

"Lachlan, *you* defeated the wicked faerie?" Ada asked in disbelief.

"Oh, it wasn't much. I just stepped on her," he said humbly.

"She'd accidentally turned herself into an ant," Kron explained.

"Thanks to you," Bia pointed out.

"I see you broke the curse," the faerie queen said to Bia.

"Yes, I understand now," she said.

"Well, I suppose you'll want to grow

taller," the faerie said to Kron.

"Actually, I've changed my mind," he said. "I believe I'm content the way I am."

"Very good." The faerie queen nodded. "Now, Lachlan, since you are the one who freed me from Miriam's power, you can have three wishes, within reason of course."

Lachlan looked around, thinking. He considered using two wishes to help his friends, but they all seemed, as Kron had put it, content the way they were.

"Now that Miriam is gone, will the forest be good again?" he asked.

"Yes, it was her magic that made it treacherous," the faerie queen answered.

That ensured that everyone would make it back without any trouble.

"Elric, Ada, would you like to be shorter, so you can fit in better in Malmor?" he asked them. They exchanged a look of surprise.

"Well," Ada said slowly, "I really don't mind being tall as long as I have Elric. But if he wants to be short, than I will be willing to change, too."

"You know, being tall might not be so bad," Elric said. "And who knows, maybe we can help Malmor learn not to be so unyielding when it comes to things being bigger than they're used to."

"In that case," Lachlan said, "I only have one wish."

~*~

Before everyone headed out on their own, Prince Nolan insisted that they stay for the night and feast. In the end, they decided to hold the weddings there. As it turned out, there was a whole town just past the castle that Miriam had changed into a garden, and they were turned back when she died, so they invited the townsfolk and got a minister to perform the ceremony. The faerie queen fabricated the wedding dresses, one for Meleen and one for Bia, though she made Meleen's prettier and Bia didn't complain.

Ada was the Matron of Honor and

Elric the Best Man. It made an interesting sight, Ada and Elric on either side of the wedded, with Kron and Bia on the left, Nolan and Meleen in the middle, and two komodo dragons on the right. Nobody noticed the reflection in the mirror on the side of the room, showing the same scene except for one couple, who appeared as a boy and a princess. And they all lived happily ever after.

The End

Cast of Characters

Prince Elric, the giant – "Clumsy, uncoordinated, slow-learning Elric was destined to become king of an entire country."

Princess Adelaide "Ada," the bride – "Though she wasn't quite as tall as the average Regallan, Elric guessed that she would come up to his shoulder, which was extraordinarily tall compared to the other Malmors he had seen."

Pem Puk, the puzzle – "Could he really be so naïve?"

Lachlan, the talkative attendant – "Lachlan quickly fit in with the boys, getting into all sorts of mischief – all in fun, of course."

Meleen, the un-talkative attendant – "Meleen remained shyly to herself most of the time."

Raja, the dragon – "She was surprisingly polite for a reptile."

Leilani, the dysfunctional faerie –

"'She's allergic to faerie dust.'"

Superbia "Bia," the magic mirror – "'As you can also undoubtedly see, I am the most beautiful woman in the world.'"

Kron, the midget – "'You probably can't tell, since you're a mirror, but I'm actually a midget.'"

Miriam, the villain – "'She's always coveted my position as queen of the faeries.'"

Gloriana, the faerie queen – "'The faerie queen is distinguished from the other faeries by her tail. She is the only faerie privileged to have one.'"

Prince Nolan, the stone prince – "The man was even more handsome as a human."

We hope you enjoyed reading
Faerie Tail by Becca Bates.

To find more exciting and engaging books, please
visit Indie Artist Press at
www.indieartistpress.com.

About the Author

Becca Bates was born in August 1990 in southern California. From an early age, she was an avid reader and often created stories of her own, though it wasn't until high school that she began writing her first novel.
After writing for a few years as a side hobby, her love for it grew until she decided it was her greatest passion and something worth pursuing professionally.
She is currently working on a full-length fantasy series called *The Eridan Chronicles*.
She makes her home in Fort Collins, Colorado.
You can contact Becca at her website:
http://beccabates.weebly.com